The Two and Only Kelly Twins

c 2

The Two and Only Kelly Twins

Johanna Hurwitz

illustrated by

Tuesday Mourning

CANDLEWICK PRESS

For the one and only Dubby Bogdan —
Happy birthday!
J. H.

To J. D. L. and M. J. L. With love.
T. M.

Text copyright © 2013 by Johanna Hurwitz
Illustrations copyright © 2013 by Tuesday Mourning

First edition 2013

Library of Congress Catalog Card Number 2012947732
ISBN 978-0-7636-5602-7

13 14 15 16 17 18 BVG 10 9 8 7 6 5 4 3 2 1

Printed in Berryville, VA U.S.A.

This book was typeset in Caecilia.
The illustrations were done in watercolor.

Candlewick Press
99 Dover Street
Somerville, Massachusetts 02144

visit us at www.candlewick.com

CONTENTS

Chapter One
Meet Arlene and Ilene

Arlene Kelly and Ilene Kelly were sisters. They were also twins. In fact they were identical twins. That means that they looked just alike. They both had straight brown hair, which they wore in matching short ponytails. They also both had brown eyes and wore the same style glasses. In addition, they had the same shaped noses and chins. They were the same height and the same weight. Hardly anyone, except their parents and they themselves, could tell them apart. Arlene and Ilene were seven years old on their birthday this year. But there was one difference between the girls. Arlene had been born at 11:55 p.m. on July 17th, and Ilene, who was just eight minutes younger, was born at 12:03 a.m. on July 18th.

"We must be the only identical twins who have different birthdays," said Arlene. She was proud of being a day older than her sister.

"I doubt it," said their mom.

"Don't forget: you're not really a whole day older than me," said Ilene. "You are only eight minutes older. That's hardly any time at all."

"Eight minutes is long enough to eat a sandwich," said Arlene.

"No. You would choke if you ate so fast," insisted Ilene.

"Eight minutes is long enough to make my bed," said Arlene.

"Eight minutes is not long enough to take a bath," said Ilene.

"Yes, it is," said Arlene.

"No, it's not," said Ilene. "You'd still be dirty."

"No, I wouldn't."

"Yes, you would."

"Eight minutes of arguing is enough to drive a mother crazy," said Mrs. Kelly. "Why don't you girls go outdoors and roller-skate until supper time?"

So the girls went outdoors, and in less than eight minutes, in fact in less than two minutes, they were laughing and racing each other down the street. They might argue, they might disagree, but mostly they were best friends. They knew they were lucky to always have someone nearby to play with or do their homework with or help when they were setting the table for a meal.

Of course they knew other kids. In fact, on the street where they lived, there were two other children just their age. Unfortunately they were both boys: Monty and Joey.

Luckily both boys were friendly, and the four often played together. Monty even took karate lessons with Arlene and Ilene. And Joey and Monty had been in the same first-grade class as Ilene. Still, even with other friends around, Arlene and Irene knew that being a twin was very special, and they considered themselves lucky.

All last year, there were two other sets of twins at their school. One set were sixth-grade sisters who were not identical. No one could guess that those two girls were even related, much less twins. One was tall, and one was short. One had curly hair, and one had straight. But they both had crooked teeth and wore braces. Half the girls in sixth grade wore braces, so that wasn't much of a clue. And since they didn't look alike, people tended to forget they were twins.

The other set of twins were in fifth grade.

They weren't identical, either. One was a boy and the other a girl. People tended to forget they were twins, too.

No one could forget about Arlene and Ilene. When they were born, Mrs. Kelly received dozens and dozens of matching sets of clothing. For their first four years of life, the girls always wore the same outfits. When they had finally outgrown the last of these gift items, Mrs. Kelly thought the girls would be delighted to pick out their own clothes. When she took them shopping for winter jackets, she was in for a surprise.

"My favorite color is blue," said Ilene.

"My favorite color is blue," said Arlene.

"I said it first," said Ilene. "You could pick green."

"I hate green," said Arlene. "Green is for frogs."

"How about red?" suggested Ilene.

"I hate red. Red is for ketchup. My favorite color is blue."

"You like ketchup on French fries," said Ilene.

"I'm not a French fry. I'm a girl. And my favorite color is blue."

"All right, all right," said Mrs. Kelly. "We'll buy two blue jackets."

"Yippee," Arlene sang out.

"Yippee Doodle," Ilene sang out.

"Yippee Doodle? Don't you mean 'Yankee Doodle'?" asked Arlene.

"Nope. 'Yippee Doodle' means I'm extra happy. I can *wear my* blue jacket, and I can *look* at *your* blue jacket."

"Yippee Doodle," Arlene agreed.

And that's how it went when the twins selected new pants, sweaters, shirts, caps, and mittens. Of course not everything was blue. They got brown pants and green pants as well as blue ones. And they got red-and-white-striped sweaters and white shirts with blue polka dots. But all of their clothes matched. And they always liked to wear them on the same day.

"How will anyone be able to tell you apart?" asked Mrs. Kelly, looking at her matching children.

"Can you tell us apart?" asked Arlene.

"Well, of course. I'm your mother," said Mrs. Kelly. "Your father and I have lived with you every day since you were born. I know that your voices are slightly different and your smiles are slightly different. And your father knows it, too."

"Well, if you can tell us apart, everyone else should be able to do it, too," said Ilene.

"Wouldn't it be funny if I woke up one morning and couldn't remember whether I was Ilene or Arlene?" said Arlene.

Ilene started laughing. "We could pretend to be each other," she suggested.

"No way," said Arlene. "I like being me. I like being Arlene."

"That's okay," said Ilene shrugging. "I like being Ilene."

"Good. That's settled," said Mrs. Kelly.

Chapter Two
Two Pets for Two Girls

Just after the twins' seventh birthday, Mr. and Mrs. Kelly finally agreed that Arlene and Ilene were old enough to have a pet.

"I want a kitten," said Arlene.

"I want a puppy," said Ilene.

"A kitten. I said it first," said Arlene.

"No. A puppy. I said it louder," insisted Ilene.

"We can't get both," said their mother. "The animals would probably fight."

"No, they wouldn't," said Arlene.

"No, they wouldn't," agreed Ilene.

"I think your mother is right. A cat and a dog in the same house can mean trouble," said Mr. Kelly.

"Then let's get a kitten. Caroline at school has an orange cat that had babies. She said she'd give me one, and I want one that is orange, too," said Arlene.

"No fair," said Ilene. "I want a puppy."

"Puppies are lots of work," Mrs. Kelly said. "They need to be walked several times a day, even in the rain or snow. You've seen Joey. He walks his dogs as soon as he comes home from school every day. And he does it after supper, too."

"I'd love to walk a puppy," said Ilene.

"I wouldn't," said Arlene. "If we got a puppy, I'd never, ever walk it."

"I don't care," said Ilene. "I'd walk the puppy all the time."

"No," said Mr. Kelly. "A puppy grows into a dog, and this house isn't big enough for two adults, two growing girls, and a dog."

"So let's get a kitten," said Arlene, smiling at what she was sure was victory. "Even when a kitten grows into a cat, it's still smaller than a dog."

"No. Wait," Ilene said. "We could get one of those teeny-tiny dogs with the funny name.

A Chihuahua. Remember we saw a lady with one when we went to the library last week? It was so little, she had it in a canvas shopping bag with her books."

"I don't want a Chihuahua," said Arlene.

"Well, I don't want a cat," said Ilene.

"And I don't want all this arguing," said Mrs. Kelly. "Just forget what Dad and I said about getting a pet."

"But you promised us," Ilene reminded her mother.

"Yes you did," said Arlene. "You said after we finished first grade, we'd be old enough to have a pet."

"How about a tank of fish?" suggested Mr. Kelly.

"No," said Arlene and Ilene in unison.

"Well, I'm glad you girls can agree on some things," said Mrs. Kelly. "But we're not making any decisions today in any event."

So a couple of weeks went by, and all of Caroline's kittens were adopted, much to Arlene's disappointment. And Mr. and Mrs. Kelly remained firm about not getting a dog.

Then one evening Mr. Kelly came home from work carrying his briefcase, a newspaper, and a box.

"What's in there?" asked Ilene, pointing to the box. She knew that the briefcase held only boring old papers.

"It's a surprise," her father said.

"Is it for us?" asked Arlene hopefully.

"Yes. It's two pets," Mr. Kelly said. "One for each of you."

The box wasn't very big, so right away

Arlene shouted, "Kittens! You got us kittens!"

"No."

"Chihuahuas!" shouted Ilene, rushing to hug her father.

"No."

"Then what is it?" asked Arlene puzzled.

"Here's a hint. It starts with an *f*," said Mr. Kelly. "And remember, there are two of them."

The two sisters looked at each other. "We don't want fish," Arlene reminded her father.

"No fish," he said.

"Frogs?" guessed Ilene. She wrinkled her nose. Who'd want a pair of frogs for pets?

"Look," said Mr. Kelly.

Arlene and Ilene stood shoulder to shoulder and watched as their father opened the box. Inside were two skinny animals with matching white hair, small claws, and tails.

"What are they?" asked Arlene.

"Ferrets," her father said.

"Wow. Ferrets," said Ilene. "Aren't they cute?" she asked as she admired the little faces, which almost resembled those of puppies or kittens. "I never even heard of ferrets. We'll be the only kids at school with ferrets for pets," she told her sister.

"Cool," agreed Arlene. She reached out a finger to pet one of the animals.

"One of the men at my office is going to be working overseas. These ferrets belonged to his children, but the family agreed it would be too difficult to settle in a new country with these critters. So he offered them to me."

Each girl picked up one of the ferrets, and they began petting them. "He's so soft," cooed Ilene.

"I love him," said Arlene.

Mr. Kelly went back to his car and returned with a large wire cage for the new pets to live in.

"Do they have to stay in the cage all the time?" asked Ilene.

"No. Just when you're not playing with them, like when you're at school."

"What should we name them?" asked Arlene.

"Whatever you want," Mr. Kelly said. "Mr. Clifton said that they are both females."

"I don't care," said Arlene. "I want to name mine Benjamin Franklin Ferret," she announced. "And I'll call him Frankie for short."

Ilene couldn't think of a name that fast. She mumbled different names to herself, trying them out. Then she suddenly remembered something. "What is the name of that cookbook you always use?" she asked her mother.

"*The Joy of Cooking?*"

"No. The other one, that you said was a wedding present from Dad's grandmother. The author has a name that starts with F."

Mrs. Kelly thought for a moment. "Do you mean *The Fannie Farmer Cookbook?*"

"Yes," said Ilene, nodding. "My ferret will be called Fannie Farmer Ferret. That's a better name for a girl ferret," she added, making a face at her sister.

"I don't know if either of those are appropriate names for ferrets," said Mr. Kelly.

"Who knows what appropriate names for ferrets are?" said his wife.

And so that's how Frankie and Fannie came to live with Arlene and Ilene Kelly.

If truth be told, Arlene and Ilene could not

tell the ferrets apart. They didn't really know which was Frankie and which was Fannie. Like the twins themselves, they seemed identical. However, one particularly loved raisins and the other loved peanut butter on a piece of cracker.

Whichever one Arlene held she called Frankie. And whichever one Ilene picked up she called Fannie. It didn't seem to matter to the ferrets, and it didn't matter to the sisters. The girls combed the ferrets' hair, dressed them in doll clothes, cut up fruit for

them, and portioned out dry food for them, too. They cleaned out the cage often, dumping the soiled newspaper from the bottom of the cage into the garbage pail. Then they cut up fresh, dry newspapers. They both agreed that their ferrets were perfect pets.

Sometimes the ferrets escaped when Arlene and Ilene were grooming them. They jumped off of the bed and hid underneath it. Then Arlene or Ilene would get down on the floor and hunt until she found the hiding creatures.

On the Saturday before school started after summer vacation, either Frankie or Fannie ran away.

"It must be Fannie, because I'm holding Frankie," said Arlene.

"Maybe yes and maybe no," said Ilene, wishing she was the one holding a ferret and her sister was the one down on her hands and knees, looking. When ten minutes passed without success, Arlene offered to help in the search. She put the ferret she had been holding inside the cage and got down on the floor. "It's too dark to see very much," she complained.

Arlene got up and got a flashlight. She turned it on and moved it around to give herself and her sister a better view of the room. "Oh, look," she exclaimed, picking up a cap from one of their markers. "I was looking for this."

"The marker must have dried up by now," said Ilene grumpily. She stood up and stretched. Where else could she look? she wondered.

The girls' backpacks were on the floor, ready and all packed for the first day of school. Ilene picked up hers and turned it upside down. It would be wonderful if Fannie was inside. But no, only a box of crayons, two pencils, an old shirt of her father's to use as a painting smock, and a paperback book to read during quiet time. These things all fell out on the floor. Then she turned the other backpack upside down. Now there were *two* boxes of crayons, *four* pencils, *two* old shirts, and *two* paperback books on the floor. There was no sign of Fannie.

"Maybe she went to another room," suggested Arlene.

"This house is too big," Ilene whined. "We'll never find her."

"Come on. I'll help you. I'll look in the kitchen and the living room. You look in Mom and Dad's bedroom and the bathroom."

Usually Ilene didn't like it when Arlene told her what to do. But this was not a time to argue. This was the time to find Fannie.

Each girl went to her assigned rooms. They crawled on the floor and looked in every corner. Suddenly, when she slid her fingers underneath the clothes hamper in the bathroom, Ilene felt a sharp pain. She pulled out her hand, and a drop of blood fell on the floor. A moment later, out popped Fannie's head.

Ilene grabbed hold of the ferret. "You naughty, naughty girl!" she scolded the ferret. "I won't give you any raisins today."

She ran into her bedroom and put the ferret into the cage. Then she went to show her mother the wound on her finger.

It was not the first time either of the girls had been bitten. A book they had borrowed from the library warned that ferrets often nip their owners. The girls had gotten good at holding their pets in such a way that they escaped most little bites. But this was the worst bite Ilene had gotten.

Mrs. Kelly washed Ilene's finger and put some iodine on the bite. It stung for a moment, but Ilene was brave and didn't cry. Then her mother put a bandage on Ilene's finger. "You must have startled Frankie," she said. "That's why she bit you."

"Fannie," said Arlene, correcting her mother.

"If you say so," said Mrs. Kelly.

Ten minutes later, both girls were skating down the street, looking to see if their friends Monty and Joey were around. Ilene wanted to show off her wound.

Mrs. Kelly replaced the bandage with a clean one on Sunday and again on Monday. She put a fresh bandage on Ilene's finger on

Tuesday before the girls left for school. "You probably don't need to cover it any longer," she said to Ilene. But Ilene insisted.

So that's how their new classmates could tell one twin from another on the first day of school. Arlene was in Mrs. Storch's second-grade class. Ilene was in Ms. Frost's second-grade class. And it was Ilene who was wearing a bandage on her left index finger. At least for the next couple of days.

Chapter Three
Triplets!

It was quite amazing. On the first day of second grade, everyone was talking about it.

When Arlene walked into her new classroom, Caroline Marks came rushing over to report to her.

"There are *three* sets of twins in kindergarten this year," Caroline Marks told her.

"No kidding," said Arlene. "Three sets. That's amazing." She wasn't exactly happy with the news. She liked being a twin and didn't especially want to share that honor with the six new kids.

"That's nothing," Paul Asher said, pointing to a girl standing nearby. "She's a triplet!"

"A triplet?" Everyone turned to look at the girl. She was not someone who had been in kindergarten or first grade at their school.

"I don't believe it," Arlene said.

The girl turned to look at her. Then she nodded. "It's true," she said. "I have a sister in Ms. Frost's class and a brother in Mrs. Gregory's class."

"My sister, Ilene, is in Ms. Frost's class," said Arlene. "We're identical. Are you?"

"My sister and I are identical, but my brother isn't. Boys can't be identical to girls," the new girl said.

"I know that," said Arlene. "What's your name?"

"Claudia Best. And my sister is Roberta Best. We're going to be the *best* kids in this school."

Arlene looked at Claudia and scowled. Who did this girl think she was, having an identical sister and a brother as well? Best triplets! Phooey.

At that very moment, Ilene, in her new

second-grade class, was learning about Roberta Best and her sister and brother. The brother was named Simon Best. Ever since they had started school, Ilene and Arlene had been singled out as special because they were twins. Now here was this Roberta, who had not only an identical sister but a brother, too.

Ilene felt very annoyed. How could she and Arlene be considered special if there were triplets in their school? Being a twin would no longer seem like a big deal.

"I'm a triplet, too," she told Roberta when no one was nearby. Ilene didn't know why she said it. Those words just came out of her mouth. And it was worth it to see the surprised look on Roberta's face.

"Really? That's weird that there are two sets of triplets in second grade."

Ilene thought quickly. "My other sister doesn't go to this school. Only my sister Arlene," said Ilene. She didn't want to have to point out two sisters to Roberta at lunchtime.

"What's your other other sister's name?" Roberta asked.

"Marlene," said Ilene. That was easy to make up. Lots of people got confused about the similarity of the twins' names and called them things like Marlene and Carlene and Darleen.

"Let's sit next to each other," said Roberta.

Reluctantly, Ilene sat next to the new girl. She hoped Roberta didn't ask any more about Marlene, because someone might tell her there was no Marlene in the Kelly family.

Luckily Ms. Frost came into the room and everyone rushed to find a seat. The morning was filled with first-day-of-school activities: going over classroom behavior, giving out textbooks, getting consent forms to bring home for their parents, and stuff like that. Ms. Frost talked about some of the things that the students would be learning in second grade. And Mrs. Storch was doing the same things in Arlene's classroom. So it wasn't until lunchtime that the Kelly sisters and the triplets all met face-to-face.

As usual, Arlene and Ilene were wearing the same outfit. They both had on red shirts and matching pants. Claudia and Roberta were not dressed alike at all. In fact, Claudia was wearing a skirt and Roberta was wearing jeans. Their brother, Simon, had on jeans, too.

"I'm going to sit with some guys from my class," he announced, and disappeared at once.

Ilene wished there was a way that she could disappear, too.

"I'd like to meet your other sister," said Roberta to Arlene. "How come she doesn't go to this school like you two?"

Arlene's mouth dropped open with surprise.

Ilene gave her a poke.

"She's extra smart, so she goes to a very

special school for kids who are geniuses," said Ilene, thinking quickly.

"We're pretty smart, too," said Claudia.

"Not as smart as Marlene," said Ilene.

Roberta looked from Ilene to Arlene. "Does she wear matching clothes like you both do?"

Arlene might not have been as smart as the imaginary triplet sister, but she had already caught on to what Ilene was doing. "No. At her school the kids all have to wear uniforms," she said.

"Then everyone would look like they are twins or triplets or quads or something," Claudia said with a laugh.

"Yeah," said Ilene. "Well, see you around." Then she dragged Arlene to a table that only had two empty chairs.

"She thinks she's so special because she's a triplet," she grumbled. "And what's worse, with the name Best, she thinks they *are* the best."

"I know," said Arlene. "That's just the way her sister is, too."

Neither Roberta nor Claudia was shy. Considering they were new to the school, you'd think the two of them would keep together during lunch and recess. But when Roberta finished her lunch, she rushed outside to play. Claudia came over to where Arlene and Ilene were sitting.

"My sister and I would love to meet your other sister," said Claudia. "What's her name again?"

"Marlene," said Ilene.

"Doreen," said Arlene at the same time. She'd forgotten the name that Ilene had said before.

"What?" asked Claudia.

"Doreen," said Ilene.

"Marlene," said Arlene at the same time.

"There's too much noise in here," said Claudia. "Let's go outside so we can hear each other better." She put her arms around Ilene and Arlene and pulled them to the door.

Ilene looked over at Arlene. "Marlene," she whispered.

Arlene nodded.

Roberta came over to join her sister and the twins. "So, can we all get together and have a playdate?" she asked.

"Oh, yes," said Ilene, pretending to think it was a good idea. "Let's do that sometime. Maybe next month."

"Why wait so long? How about this coming Saturday?" asked Claudia. "Where do you live?"

Arlene looked helplessly at Ilene. Ilene looked scared. What had she gotten them into?

Arlene recited their address. At least she knew the answer to that question.

"But I don't think this Saturday . . . " she began to say. She was going to tell Claudia that they wouldn't be home on Saturday, but she was interrupted by the bell. Recess was over, and it was time to line up to return to class.

"It's a date," said Claudia as she went off with Arlene.

"Who would believe that there would be two sets of triplets here in our new school?" Roberta whispered to Ilene.

Ilene shrugged. Who, indeed, would believe that?

Luckily Roberta and Claudia were not walkers. They took one of the big yellow buses waiting outside of the school building. Arlene and Ilene were walkers. They joined Monty and Joey as they headed home.

"It's amazing about the triplets," said Monty.

"Yeah," Joey agreed.

"Listen," said Ilene. "We're playing a trick on Roberta and Claudia. I told them we have another sister and that we're triplets, too.

Don't let on to them that I made that up."

"You lied to them?" asked Monty.

"It's not exactly a lie," said Arlene, defending her sister. "It's more like a joke. The only trouble is they want to come to our house on Saturday, and then they'll find out the truth."

Joey started laughing. "I know how you can trick them some more," he said.

"How?" asked Arlene and Ilene together.

Even though there was no one around to overhear him, Joey leaned closer to the sisters and whispered his idea.

The children all laughed.

Ilene crossed her fingers. "I hope it works," she said. After all, she was the one who had started this joke.

Chapter Four
The Playdate

On Saturday morning, Roberta and Claudia showed up at the Kelly house. They were brought by their father, who had a long list of errands to take care of. That was good because it meant he just waved to Mrs. Kelly at the door and shouted, "I'll be back for the girls in a couple of hours." Arlene and Ilene knew that if one of their parents had dropped them off somewhere, they would have stopped to talk. Had Roberta and

Claudia's father said anything, it would quickly have come out that his daughters were visiting a pair of twins and not triplets at all.

By plan, Ilene walked over to the two girls. "Hi," she said. "I'm Marlene."

"Hi, I'm Roberta."

"And I'm Claudia," said her sister. "Where are Arlene and Ilene?"

"They're inside," said Ilene.

The three girls went into the house. Arlene was sitting on the sofa. "Hi," she called to them.

"Which one are you?" asked Roberta.

"I'm Arlene. I'm in your class," she reminded Roberta.

"Where's Ilene?" asked Claudia.

"She's upstairs. I'll tell her you're here," said Ilene/Marlene.

She ran upstairs and a minute later came back downstairs. "Hi, everybody," she called out.

"Where's your sister?" asked Claudia.

Ilene pointed to Arlene.

"No, no. Not her. The other one," said Claudia.

"I think she went to the bathroom."

"Why don't we play something?" suggested Arlene. "How about hide-and-seek?"

"Who's going to be it?" asked Roberta.

"I'll get Marlene and tell her she's it," said Ilene.

She ran upstairs and then came down again.

"Okay," she said. "I like to be it."

"But where's Ilene?" asked Claudia.

"She went to the bathroom."

"Are you girls sick or something?" asked Roberta.

"Why?"

"Well, you keep having to go to the bathroom," she said.

"Don't be silly," said Arlene. "Everyone has to go to the bathroom sometime. Okay, Marlene. Cover your eyes and we'll all hide."

So Ilene/Marlene leaned against the wall and put her hands over her eyes. She began to count slowly to twenty-five. "Ready or not, here I come! Anyone around my base is it!" she shouted when she reached the last number.

None of the girls were around. Ilene was relieved to be able to just sit down on the sofa. She was exhausted from running up and down the stairs, pretending to be Marlene. In fact, she no longer remembered who she was at that moment. Was she Ilene or Marlene?

She got up and walked toward the stairs.

"Home free!" called a voice. It was Roberta.

Ilene started upstairs to look for the other girls. When she was midway up the stairs, she heard Arlene's voice: "Home free!"

Only one more person to find. She walked into her bedroom. Sitting on the floor was Claudia. She seemed to have forgotten the game, because she was poking her fingers through the cage at Frankie and Fannie.

"What are these?" she asked.

"Ferrets," explained Ilene. "We couldn't agree on a puppy or a kitten. So in the end we got these. They're lots of fun."

Ilene opened the cage and put one of the ferrets into Claudia's lap.

"Oh, I love it," said Claudia. "I bet Roberta and Simon would, too. Maybe we can get some ferrets once we're settled in at our house. Right now half our stuff is still in boxes. It's taking longer to unpack than it took us to pack for our move here."

"Ferrets love hiding in boxes," said Ilene. "They climb in and out of everything. Once Fannie got inside the comforter cover, and it took us hours to find her. In the end, my mom discovered a suspicious lump. And there she was!"

"Hey, where are you?" called Arlene. She came into the room, followed by Roberta.

"Did you forget we were playing a game?"

"Ohhh. What are those?" asked Roberta.

"These are ferrets," said Claudia. "Here." She held Fannie out to Roberta. "See how soft she is."

Soon all four girls were sitting on the floor, playing with the ferrets. It was lots of fun until Ilene remembered that there was supposed to be another sister. She wondered whether it would be Claudia or Roberta who noticed that someone was missing. Both guests seemed very busy studying the ferrets. Claudia was looking at a book Mr. Kelly had bought at the pet shop that told lots of facts about the animals. Roberta was looking over her shoulder.

Finally, Ilene could bear it no longer. "Listen up," she said. "I have to tell you something."

Roberta, Claudia, and Arlene turned to look at Ilene.

"It's about Marlene," she said.

"Who?" asked Roberta.

"Marlene. Our other sister. She isn't here."

"Where is she?" asked Claudia with a big grin. "Did she go away?"

"Yes," said Arlene. "She's not here now."

"Or ever," said Ilene sheepishly. "I made her up."

"You mean she just lives in your imagination?" suggested Roberta.

Ilene nodded.

"I guessed it," she said.

"How?"

"First of all, there aren't enough beds in your house. I counted when I was hiding. There was no place for Marlene to sleep."

"And besides, you couldn't even agree on what was her name when you were talking about her at school," added Claudia.

"It was just a joke," said Arlene.

"Did we fool you at all?" asked Ilene.

"Maybe for about five seconds," admitted Roberta.

"It doesn't matter," said Claudia. "There are enough of us to have a good time together. You don't need another sister for us to play with."

"Poor Simon," Roberta commented. "We can do some things together at home. But he doesn't like a lot of the stuff we do. He won't play beauty parlor or dress-up. But we can play card games and Monopoly and things like that. It's too bad we aren't quadruplets: two girls and two boys. That would be most fair for him."

"He'll probably make friends at school," said Arlene.

"If you bring him the next time you come here, he could play with Monty and Joey. They live on our street, and they're both in second grade, just like us," suggested Ilene. She was about to admit that fooling the girls had been Joey's idea, but then she thought the better of it.

Just then Fannie Farmer jumped out of

Roberta's hands. She slipped under the bed, and the four girls focused their attention on finding her. Sometimes the ferrets were hard to catch. It was a good thing that there were only two and not three of them.

Chapter Five
Which Witch Is Which?

It was hard for Arlene and Ilene to decide
what their favorite day of the year was.

When their birthday was approaching,
both girls were sure that July 17 and July 18
were the best days. Those days were filled
with gifts, a party, ice cream and cake, and
the satisfaction of being a whole year older
from one day to the next.

But what about Christmas? Their mom
always baked loads of special holiday

cookies, which she traded with a group of friends. Suddenly the house would be filled with different cook-ies shaped like trees and stars and other holiday items. They were frosted in holiday colors and topped with silver balls or multicolored sprinkles. Then there was the excitement of giving and receiving presents, TV specials, visits from family members, and vacation from school.

"I love Valentine's Day," Ilene remembered.

Arlene thought for a moment. "Me too," she agreed. "I love those pink heart cookies that Mom makes."

"I love getting valentines."

"I got more than you last year," Arlene claimed.

"That's because your teacher had everyone make cards in class to give out to all the other kids."

"We had a class post office," Arlene remembered. "I wonder if we'll do that now."

"Probably not," said Ilene. "Don't forget, we're in second grade. We're not studying about community helpers like the letter carriers and the people who work at the post office."

Arlene nodded. "Anyhow, Valentine's Day is a long way off," she said. "Now is the time to think about Halloween."

"I love Halloween!" said Ilene.

"Me too," agreed Arlene. "We'll have costumes, and we'll go trick-or-treating."

"I love trick-or-treating."

"Me too."

Ilene remembered the bag of candy she

collected last year when she was dressed as a princess.

Arlene had been a princess, too, but her costume looked very different from her sister's. Arlene had worn a long pink dress, and Ilene had had a long blue one. Their mother had made them both from old sheets.

"What do you want to be this year?" Ilene asked her sister.

"I want to be a witch."

"A witch!" cried Ilene. "Me, too. I'll be a witch, too."

"I said it first," Arlene reminded her sister.

"I said it loudest," said Ilene. "Besides, lots of kids dress like witches. We can both do it."

Arlene thought for a moment. "Okay," she agreed. "We'll both be witches, but I did say it first."

"I said it last, but it doesn't matter."

They ran off to tell their mother the good news. "We want to be witches for Halloween," they both shouted together.

"Let me see what I can do," Mrs. Kelly said. Halloween was not her favorite holiday. There were the arguments with her daughters about how many pieces of their Halloween loot they could eat after supper each evening. She thought one was a good number. The girls thought ten was better.

Last year she had said, "Let's compromise. How about two pieces each?"

Neither Arlene or Ilene had known about the principle of compromise, but they had figured it out quickly.

"How about nine pieces?" said Arlene.

"Absolutely not," said Mrs. Kelly. "You will rot your teeth."

"Eight pieces?" said Ilene.

"No, no, no," said Mrs. Kelly.

"Seven pieces," pleaded Arlene.

"That's still too many. You are going to make yourselves sick," their mother said.

In the end, it was agreed that the girls could have three pieces each. But not one piece more.

Mrs. Kelly went to a fabric store in town

and purchased a few yards of cheap black cloth. Then she set to work making outfits for her daughters.

"We're lucky not to have triplets or quadruplets," she told her husband.

"You're lucky that Halloween only comes once a year," he reminded her.

On October 31st, the costumes were ready. Arlene and Ilene put on their outfits and admired each other. It was better than looking in a mirror.

The girls had arranged with other kids on their street to go trick-or-treating together after supper. Besides Monty and Joey, there was also a girl named Lucy who was in fourth grade and lived on the corner. There were two brothers, in fourth and fifth grade, named Hank and Mike who lived on the far end in the opposite direction. All together they represented two witches, a bride, an astronaut, a cowboy, a ghost, and a monster.

Joey's mom had agreed to accompany the children, and Mrs. Kelly said she would, too. Mr. Kelly was going to stay home to open the door to any other trick-or-treaters. Children often came from neighboring streets with bags they hoped to fill with candy. There was a box of treats waiting to be given out.

"Seven children coming to a door at once seems a bit much," Mrs. Kelly said when

they were all together at the corner. "I think we should split up. Half of the children can come with me and we'll do this street. And the other half can go with Mrs. Thomas around the corner. Then we'll switch streets and ring the bells of the other people."

"Girls," Mrs. Kelly said to her daughters, "I think you should split up. No need for two witches to arrive at someone's house at the same time."

"Okay," said Arlene. "It really doesn't matter. We're all going to the same homes, and we'll all be getting the same stuff."

So Joey, Monty, and Ilene went off in the dark with Mrs. Thomas.

And Arlene, Lucy, Hank, and Mike went with Mrs. Kelly.

Off they went. At the first house, while Mrs. Thomas waited on the sidewalk, they rang the doorbell. A mother holding an infant in her arms opened the door.

"Trick or treat!" the three children shouted.

The mother was prepared. She dropped two miniature chocolate bars in each of the bags that were held out to her. "Just think," she said. "In a few years, my little Peter John will be out trick-or-treating with you."

Ilene wasn't sure about that, but she kept her mouth closed. By the time Peter John was four years old, she would be in sixth grade and in middle school. She might be too old to go trick-or-treating by then.

At the next house, a short, bald man had a large bowl of pennies. He put his hand in the bowl and then dropped a few coins in each bag.

"Pennies." Ilene made a face as they walked away. "You can't buy anything with pennies."

"It depends how many you have," Monty pointed out.

Soon the bags were filled with chocolates, miniature candy bars, small boxes of raisins, lollipops, coins, and chewing gum. There were other groups of children walking down the street, too. Because of the costumes and the masks that some of them wore, they couldn't recognize one another. They didn't live on this street, but it didn't matter. Ilene's group reached the end of the block just as Mrs. Kelly came with the trick-or-treaters she had been accompanying.

"How much do you have?" Arlene asked her sister as they met up.

"It's great," Ilene said. "Every single person opened the door." She was remembering last year, when some doors had remained shut. Either no one was home or someone was inside but pretending not to be there. It wasn't a very friendly way to behave on Halloween, but that's how some people were.

Mrs. Kelly waited on the sidewalk while Arlene, accompanied by the monster, the ghost, and the bride, rang the first doorbell.

"Trick or treat!" the children called out as the door opened.

The white-haired woman who answered looked at the characters before her. She put a candy bar into the monster's bag, the ghost's bag, and the bride's bag. She didn't give anything to Arlene.

"You forgot me," Arlene said.

"No," the woman said sharply. "You have enough. I can't give you anything more."

"That's not very nice," Lucy the bride said to Arlene.

"Maybe she's running out of candy," Arlene said. She made a point of pushing her way in front of the others when they rang the next doorbell.

"You again!" said a teenage girl. She put a lollipop in each bag but ignored Arlene.

"What about me?" asked Arlene.

"Don't be so piggy," the teenager said, and she banged the door shut.

It wasn't until the third house, where again

she was denied any treats, that Arlene and her mother realized what was happening. "Everyone thinks you've been to their house already because you look exactly like Ilene," Mrs. Kelly said.

"That's not fair," protested Arlene.

"You're right," her mother agreed. "I'll explain at the next house."

So she did, and Arlene got her share of candy but also a few suspicious looks.

"People on this street don't know you have a twin sister," Mrs. Kelly said. "Maybe next year, you and Ilene can pick out different costumes."

In the end, everyone received a large assortment of candies. And even though Ilene had also been turned down by some people, Mrs. Kelly said the two girls should pool all their treats. Together they would have more than anyone.

Instead of going off to still another street, Mrs. Kelly invited everyone to come home with her. The children sat down and examined the stuff in their bags.

"Who wants to trade me their gum for this box of raisins?" asked Hank.

Soon there was a lot of trading going on.

Meanwhile, Mr. Kelly filled a tub with water. Then the children bobbed for apples.

Before long there was a damp bride, astronaut, cowboy, monster, ghost, and pair of witches eating the apples they had succeeded in getting. Then, since it was getting late, they each took their bag of goodies to go home. At the door, Mrs. Kelly added a small tube of toothpaste to the contents of each bag.

"This is a weird treat," said the monster. The others all agreed.

"Not at all," said Mrs. Kelly. "You need to brush your fangs after you eat your candy," she told him.

When everyone was gone, Arlene said, "Next year I want to be a ballerina."

"Me too!" shouted Ilene.

"I said it first," said Arlene.

"I said it loudest,"said Ilene.

"I say get out of your wet clothes and get

ready for bed," said Mrs. Kelly. "Next Hallow-een is a long way off. You have plenty of time to figure out what you want to be."

"Soon it will be Christmas!" remembered Arlene.

"I love Christmas!" shouted Ilene.

"Don't forget Thanksgiving," said Mr. Kelly, walking into the room.

"I love Thanksgiving," said Arlene.

"I love Thanksgiving!" shouted Ilene.

"I said it first," said Arlene.

"I said it loudest!" said Ilene.

"I said it's bedtime," said Mrs. Kelly. She said it first *and* she said it loudest, so the two witches went to get ready for bed.

Chapter Six
The Separation

On November second, just two days after Halloween, Arlene woke in the middle of the night. She had a terrible pain in her stomach, and she felt like throwing up. She called out to her mother.

"I'm sick," she moaned.

Ilene was sound asleep and didn't hear anything at first. But as Arlene continued calling, Ilene gradually woke up.

"Keep quiet," she mumbled to her sister. "I'm trying to sleep."

Luckily, Arlene's cries had awakened her mother as well as Ilene.

"What's the matter, honey?" asked a groggy Mrs. Kelly.

"My stomach hurts," Arlene said.

"I'm not surprised. It's all that candy you've been eating. Anyone would be sick."

"I'll never eat a piece of candy again," moaned Arlene. She jumped out of bed and went rushing to the bathroom. A moment later, she threw up.

Mrs. Kelly took a damp washcloth and cleaned Arlene's face. "You feel a little warm, too. I bet you have a fever." She gave Arlene a cup of water. "Rinse out your mouth. It will make you feel better."

"I feel awful," Arlene said.

"Do you need to throw up again?" asked her mother.

"I don't know."

"Here," said Mrs. Kelly, taking the plastic wastebasket from the bathroom. "I'll put this by your bed in case you need it. Just lie down. You'll probably feel better in the morning."

Arlene lay down in bed, but she felt too terrible to sleep. She felt like throwing up, but nothing came out. She couldn't remember ever having felt so awful in her whole life. After a few minutes, she went to her parents' bedroom. "Can you dial 911?" she begged her mother. "I think I'm dying."

Both of Arlene's parents sat up in bed. Mr. Kelly turned on the light.

"She looks awful," he said to his wife.

"I feel awful," said Arlene.

"It's two in the morning," said Mrs. Kelly.

"Can we call the doctor at this hour?"

"Why not?" said Arlene's father. "She won't answer the phone. All the doctors have phone services, and they'll advise us on what to do."

After a call to the service and a call back from the doctor, Arlene was in her parents' car wrapped in a blanket and on her way to the emergency room at the hospital. Ilene, who didn't have a stomachache, was also wrapped in a blanket in the backseat of the car.

"We couldn't leave you at home alone, honey," Mrs. Kelly apologized. Ilene nodded. She was half asleep. She woke at the hospital and then curled up on a couch in the waiting area. It was lumpy, not comfortable like her bed. Still, she dozed off and on. When she woke, at six a.m., she didn't even know where she was. The whole night had seemed like a dream to her.

The whole night had seemed like a nightmare to Arlene. She was examined and given a couple of tests by the hospital staff. Then she was assigned a bed in the children's area and had to wait for her doctor to come. It seemed Arlene had appendicitis and would need surgery.

There was a discussion about whether one of her parents should take Ilene home for breakfast and to put on clothing. She couldn't go to school in her pajamas.

Ilene yawned. "Where's Arlene?" she asked.

"She's waiting to see Dr. Clive," said Mrs. Kelly.

Ilene yawned again.

"Why does Ilene have to go to school?" Mr. Kelly asked his wife. "She looks like she needs more sleep after the night we've just had."

So that day both Arlene and Ilene stayed home from school. After Mrs. Kelly called the school to explain her daughters' absence, a rumor quickly went around the second grade. Identical twins Arlene and Ilene Kelly both were having their appendixes removed.

It seemed amazing. They always did everything alike.

But only Arlene had her appendix removed. And it was decided that she should remain at the hospital for at least a couple of days. That meant that Ilene slept in her room at home all alone that night. She had never slept in a room alone before in her entire life. Still, it was fun playing with both ferrets by herself. She wondered if Frankie missed Arlene. Maybe she was like all the humans they knew and couldn't tell the twins apart, either.

In his bedroom, her father was alone, too. The hospital had a special folding bed that Mrs. Kelly could sleep on so that Arlene wouldn't be alone and sad away from home.

The next morning, Ilene walked to school without having her sister by her side. She had never walked to school alone, or in fact done much of anything alone, in her entire seven years. The twins had never been separated before.

Ilene wasn't exactly alone. Her friends Monty and Joey walked with her.

"Poor Arlene," said Monty. "How is she feeling?"

"I guess she's okay now that the operation is over," said Ilene.

Even though Monty and Joey were friends of the twins, it felt strange to Ilene to be walking with them and not to have Arlene along, too.

At school, she thought about Arlene all morning long. Her father had told her that Arlene would still not be home when school let out. At lunchtime, the second-graders were always permitted to sit with the children from the other second-grade classes. Every day Ilene and Arlene rushed to sit together. Today Ilene was alone. But right away, two girls from Arlene's class came and joined her.

"I guess you miss your sister," said one.

"What do you have for lunch?" asked the other.

Ilene opened her lunch box. There was a tuna-fish sandwich and an apple cut into quarters. There was also a little box of raisins from her Halloween treats. Both of the other girls discovered they had boxes of raisins in their lunches, too. It made them laugh. They talked together, and Ilene stopped thinking about Arlene for a little while. The girls jumped rope together during recess.

Just before dismissal time, a girl from Arlene's class came to Ilene's classroom. She delivered an envelope filled with get-well cards made by her classmates. Ilene stuffed the envelope into her backpack. She walked home with Monty and Joey.

"Are you going to karate this afternoon?" Monty asked.

Ilene had never gone to karate class without Arlene.

"Maybe," she said. "Maybe not."

"We'll miss you if you don't come," said Monty. "It'll be bad enough that Arlene won't be there. Please come," he begged.

"Okay," Ilene agreed. It was nice that Monty wanted her to go with him.

Karate was fun. Ilene learned a new movement that day. She would have to teach it to Arlene when she came home from the hospital. That way she wouldn't fall behind.

All the next day, Ilene wondered what time Arlene would get home. Would she come in the morning while Ilene was doing math? Or maybe she'd come home in time to have lunch with their mother. Ilene imagined her sister eating and talking and laughing with their mother. She wished she was there with them. Maybe they'd watch something on TV together when lunch was over. Or maybe they'd play a game. Ilene sighed as she did her math problems.

When Ilene got home that afternoon, there was Arlene. She was sitting on the sofa in the living room and wearing new pajamas. They didn't match any that Ilene had. Arlene also had several gifts: two new books, a puzzle, and a huge container of chocolate kisses. On the coffee table was a pile of get-well cards. How did so many people know that Arlene had been in the hospital? Ilene wondered.

It all reminded Ilene of a book their mother

had read to them when they were little. Madeline had her appendix out, too, and she also got lots of presents. But unlike the children in that story, Ilene didn't think she wanted to have her appendix out.

Monty came over with a plate of home-made chocolate-chip cookies. "My mom made these for Arlene, but you can have some, too," he told Ilene. "When will Arlene go back to school?" Monty wanted to know.

"Mom says I can go back on Monday," Arlene told him.

Monty looked at the new puzzle that Arlene had. "Can we do it together?" he asked.

It seemed like a good idea. So Arlene and Ilene and Monty began work on the puzzle. It was a hard one. It had two hundred pieces.

While they worked on the puzzle, the children ate some of the chocolate kisses.

Even Arlene ate some, although just a couple of nights ago, she had said she'd never eat candy again.

"Either you have a very short memory or you are feeling much better," said Mrs. Kelly when she walked into the living room to check on Arlene.

When it was time for Monty to go home for his supper, the puzzle was still unfinished. "I can come over tomorrow and help some more," he offered. Then he looked at the two sisters and said, "You aren't identical twins now."

"Yes, we are," said both Arlene and Ilene together.

Monty shook his head no. "You might look alike. You have the same hair and glasses and stuff, but you're not identical anymore," he insisted.

"Why? Because we're not wearing matching clothes?" asked Ilene.

"No. Because Arlene is missing her appendix and Ilene still has an appendix."

Both girls started laughing. They were alike and not alike at the same time. But the difference was a secret that no one could see just by looking at them.

"I missed you," Arlene told Ilene when they were in bed that night.

"I missed you, too," Ilene told her sister. "But," she confessed, "I still had a good time at school and at karate."

"I made friends with a girl in the next bed at the hospital," Arlene admitted. "Neither of us ate the string beans on our supper trays yesterday. Maybe when she's feeling better, I'll go over to her house to visit her."

"I made friends with two girls from your class," Ilene said. "We ate lunch together and played during recess."

"Twins don't have to do everything together every minute," said Arlene.

"I know," said Ilene nodding in the dark.

"Still, we're lucky to have each other," said Arlene.

"Yes," Ilene agreed. She put her head down on her pillow, and in one minute, she was sound asleep.

And just alike, so was Arlene.